Colorful Thoughts

Jonessi

ISBN:

DEDICATION

Me, Myself and I

ACKNOWLEDGMENTS

I want to thank everyone or everything that is around me that gave me
inspiration and ideas to write my own poetry

Breath of

Slow, Hard, Silent, Loud breaths

Chest caving, sharp pains

High and low chest movements

Steady yourself and try to ease the channel

Whatever it is; keep your body and mind at a slower pace

Don't overload the breathing technique

Confused

Is this real or make believe

Be the judge and count your opinion as judge or juror

Fantasy real or make believe

Just because you don't act on it does it still feel make believe or real

Some things you won't experience is that real or fake

Do you have to act out on everything that is in your thoughts and dreams

If you do those things and tell your friends will they believe you or say you're a liar

Why does that have to be a defining moment

Just because it may seem impossible does it really matter

Am I taking in circles or are you getting lost in my circles

If you have an imagination then you'll understand

It may seem fake to you but real to me

Thoughts are provocative, enticing, complex, funny and any other adjectives that I can't think of

It's how you perceive them and what you do with it

Is it real or make believe

Creativity at its best

Stop, Pause, Think, Realize

Breath, Exhale, Repeat

Stop, Pause, Think, Wonder

Breath, Exhale, Repeat

Stop, Pause, Think, Relax

Breath, Exhale, Repeat

Demons

Past may haunt you but it is an essential part of growth

It steers through the good, bad and ugly times of existence

It is a GPS in the vast life

Reminders of what not to do and the mistakes

Reminders of the good times and how to cope with change

Ugly truth that should be embraced like that Christmas sweater or hairstyle

Sets a part of who you're trying to be now from then

Another voice whoever is may be is there listening, chiming in urging you to try and succeed whatever it is even if bad or good failure

Willing to ask for help or will you let it consume you

Some are not going to understand the pressure

Some will say it is human nature

Why are you doing this or seeing this person(s) or asking some else

Don't let that stop you

Reclaim what is yours

Rejoice when you find your way again

Faith

What do you believe

What do you see in the clouds

When you're happy does the sun shine brighter when you come outside

When your sad does it pour

When you're angry does the thunder rumble

Faith: Reincarnation

Do you come back as a flower, tree, ant or whatever

Does my spirit go unrest and watch over you

Faith: Inner thoughts

Does what you believe in outweigh what the next person believe in

The funny thing is it doesn't matter

What does your heart feel

Doesn't your blood run the same was as mine

Don't we bleed the same color

Don't we all have questions and uncertainties

Are we perfect

Faith cont.

Faith: Culture

The beauty is to have a colorful perspective form all cultures far and wide

That we all are loved no matter what group we are a part

First Love

You took me places I've never been

You were the one to open my eyes to love

I started believing in romance and became a hopeless romantic because of you

You stole, broke and repaired my heart

I realize that it may seem strange but through the ups and downs you'll always be the one that has my heart

I will always love you no matter what

Growth

Growing tall, big and strong as parent and doctors say

Growing hair, nails, toes, arms, breast, butt, mind within

Situations throughout the years

How do you handle the growing pains

It doesn't matter the way you grow blowing in the wind, the straight and narrow, the wild child, the Rebellious; whichever way

Matters the dealing of the cards, obstacles and the take from it

H&P

Flowing stream of devotion

A vessel of love and pain

Sometimes you listen with the wrong intention

Guidance shouldn't be lead unless you include an important part

Pumping blood flow

Bestowed the tightness and elasticity

Beautiful interaction among the sexes

Raw uncut purity

Precious commodity

A flawed jewel that no one understands

Is it used the right or wrong way or is it being wasted away

Still there is something missing

Dissing the most important part

Understand what it needs and takes to blossom

Eventually the understand will arise

Happiness

What is happiness to you

Is it all the good things in your life

Is it all the good and bad things that affects you

Is it when you feel strong and healthy

Is it a smile and when someone smiles back

Is it a laugh when something is funny

Have you ever thought of happiness as a wrong turn

What about a misstep or miscue

How does a person determine happiness or something good happening majority of the time

It is a degree of miscues, wrong turns, falling down, sadness, worries and a little of smiles and encouragement

The very definition may be various to some

Happiness may be explained in many different views and perspectives

Will you see the happiness in any form or shape is the question

Human Nature

Humans do the unthinkable

Don't ever underestimate no one

Realize we all talk about one another (good or bad)

Realize we all have courage, strength, weakness,

    love, sensual/crazy, wild side, etc.

    Think about it some strengths are stronger than others

Test those parts of your anatomy

Mindsets and physical body various in all of us

Don't be afraid of that animal instinct inside

Ignorance is Bliss

Why is that person happy not knowing what the future may bring
Are they content on being in that bubble and not exploring

What do they gain in being limited

Is that person sad, happy, angry to not know what their purpose is

Do they want to move but feel trapped of not knowing what is in store

Do they harm themselves for not pushing to learn more or being
manipulated by some considered to wiser than them

Does society gain in folks not knowing/ignoring to help the people in
the world

Is it good to act like you don't know something to move in social status

Does mindlessly people gain more in emotions not having to feel the
anguish, pain, etc.

How does it help and when should you flip the switch to knowing or not
knowing or being blind to it all

When is not knowing helpful and acceptable in the matter of affairs,
heart, etc.

Imagination

Mind traveling at warp speed

Colorful, Black and White, Real time

Ideas flowing with validity

CEO, entrepreneurship, co-worker, assistant, supervisor

Creativity that blossoms with every thought

Trials and Tribulations

Some that make sense and some that don't

Missing some research and money to capitalize on those dreams

Some memories that you remember and those if you don't write down then lose forever

Stop and Focus

Every admiration will flow but have to take one step at time

One thought focus and others to follow

Humorous, Weird, Really what was that about

Sometimes would like to get the thoughts analyze and wonder what Freud or Jung would say

Mind traveling at warp speed

Colorful, Black and White, Real time

Inhibition

Toys, videos, creams, lotions

Clothing, semi, naked

Slow, fast, steady

Saddle, chair, bed, wall

Heavy, light, no screams

Glistening, glowing

Peachy, funky

Passion, love, frustration

Unfiltered, Over-the-top, simplified

Boring, exciting, modest joy

Knowing, not knowing, curiosity

Thoughts, fantasy, reality

Interpretation of Bare Necessity

Water Food Clothing

Smiles Laughter Cries

Some A Lot None

Walmart Target Goodwill

Nordstrom Macy's Gucci

Simple Modest Ginormous

Plain In-between Over-top

Make

Break

Kindness

Treat others the same as they treat you

Laugh and enjoy the humor in everyone

Smile when they look at you funny

Laugh and smile when they get smart

Be honest when you speak the truth

Laugh when they make you angry because they don't know any better

Laugh at it all because life, people, job will always be same shit just another day

Kindness is something that kills people

Laughing at people pisses them off and keep you balance

Kindness keeps the stress level down

Everything balances out and the laughter keeps you from crying or being down in dumps

Kindness is the best medicine and a powerful tool even though it may be difficult

See how far kindness takes you

Of course don't think it makes you weak

Laughter

Giggles, Smiles, Sounds

Large, Medium, Small

Unbelievable facial expressions

Needed to calm the soul

And release the everyday pressure of life

It keeps the tears away

Unless your giggles are too strong and it makes you cry (that's a good thing)

Giggling so hard you almost pee your pants

We all need laughter

It's the joy of happiness, funniest times in life

Memories that you always want to remember

Memories that put that funny face with strange sounds coming from the mouth and sometimes the occasionally nose snort

Have you laughed today

Maybe you should at least once a day

Therapeutic

Mother

A caregiver for her immediate family and friends

A friend

A therapist

A coach

A doctor

A monster catcher

A storyteller

A musician

A banker

A designer

A hustler

An author

A problem solver

A teacher

A mother is many things however you may see what she does for you

The title is endless

Let it stand tall because we don't need a definition

MOTHER

Power

Hidden inhibition within yourself has to be explored

What stimulated the thoughts that flow inside you

Is it the drive to shine at whatever

Do you relate to the same masses or indifference

Suggestive behavior to advance in any place

Does the consumption takeover to lead instead of follow or follow instead of lead

When should it be turned on or off

Light has timing and so does the sun

Dark has its timing and so does the moon

Balance is the key but know when to weigh in

Pressure or Sexual Tensions

Heavy burden on your shoulders

Pressure mounting on the brain, heart, and anywhere in between

Pushing past the masses to make it everyday

Content on your face to mask any revealing emotions

Smiling until it hurts

Crying until you can't produce anymore tears

Aging with everyday unhappiness

Grays taking over your hair and the dying to conceal

Stop and deal with the mounting hill of life

Will you let it guide your or set you backwards in time

Reality Television

Tall, Short, Big, small

Children or no children

Does it matter if your r$ch or poor

Do you really need big breast or

butts?

Do you know your self-worth?

Do you love yourself?

Does these things make you truly happy?

Will they sag over time?

Should you really care what you're supposed to look like?

Expected or Pressured; as long as your healthy a big factor?

Is it okay to eat right but have pie, cake or ice cream every once in a while?

Am I different because of the color of my skin, sexuality, hair (kinky, straight, curly – whatever type)?

Reality Television cont.

Should I be treated different because of my body image?

Why are you intimidated by my intelligence and that I have a mind?

Accept me for who I am?

Because I DO!!!!

Am I supposed to act ratchet, hood, ghetto fabulous, prissy and uppity to get you to notice me?

What is wrong with my accent?

Do I need to have a story line just to get or be notice on social media, etc.?

Why can't you see me without the cameras, the phone, twitter, YouTube, Instagram, and Facebook?

Why do you need to know my every move?

Make-up, No make-up?

Stylist, No stylist?

 Fake or Real?

Do you recognize the real me?

Would you not recognize the real me in person?

Do I even recognize me in the mirror?

Sex Sexual Relations Love F$$$ing

Toys Videos Creams Lotions

Clothing Semi Naked

Slow Fast Steady

Saddle Chair Bed Wall

Heavy Light Screams

Glistening and Glowing

Peachy Funky

Passion Love Frustration

Unfiltered Over the top Simplified

Boring Exciting (think of another word)

Knowing Not-Knowing Curiosity

Thoughts Fantasy Reality

Sexy

Does my outline appease you

Do you like the tall slender me

Or the short thick me

Do you like the in between me

Should it matter the outline or silhouette you see

Kissing you in the spot that drives you wild

Undressing you with my eyes

Shyness that I act when we're in public

Touching your skin, the warmth radiating underneath

Walking to the beat that sets you on fire

Sashaying my hips to the rhythm

Moist with inner desire

Feline within showcasing my strength

Glowing with inhibition and presence of mind

Accept, Embrace the prowess within me

Always showcase that vibe in the gracious, bad, good, rough, tired or in between days

Sexy cont.

It won't fade or disappear

Stronger it becomes within your journey

Take it from me the average maiden

Embrace yourself prowess or the powerful self within

Smile ☺

Show me those teeth; don't be ashamed of how they look

Show me those lines; not matter if your face cracks

Don't you know you have pretty smile who cares what others think

Do you like your smile; even if it does look awkward and sometimes you close your eyes

Smile **BIG** Smile W   I   D   E

Practice that camera ready everyday smile in the mirror if you have to

Smile for me now

Speaking your mind

Express my feelings

Why am I perceived differently to you

Does my use of words terrify you

Don't I speak with clarity and precision

Tone and pitch evolves

Or is silence better

Does it scare you that I can express myself verbally and non-verbally

Point is always perceived

Not my problem that you can't handle my non-verbal or verbal self

Deal with it

Timeout

Do you require a timeout corner

There is one if you didn't know

But will you make the time

This corner by the wall helps us all

Self-reflection is why you're in that corner

Have you learned what was meant of you

Do you need more time in that corner

Yes, you do because the message isn't or yet received

Maybe, I'll add headphone to block out the noise

You don't need to hear what everybody else is doing

Sit in that corner and be still or don't move

As if time has stopped

Stop trying to come out the corner

You're there for a reason

Message isn't yet perceived

Sit in that corner and be still

Timeouts are requirements in life

Understanding

What do you want from me?

What do you want from me.

What do you want from me…..

What do you want from me!

If you don't know or understand

How do you expect me to help you get there to understand me

Think about what you want and truly understand the aspects of it all before you demand something from me

What do you want from me?

What is anguish…?

Is it the hurt you feel towards others that treat you wrong

Do you feel it when you listen to that sad song?

Why does ever your family do you wrong

Why do you lose some friends along the way?

People are supposed to be different because that is what makes us unique

We don't have to get along or sing Kumbaya

Let's work on the common sense; Instead of chopping up ideas like mince

The green you see is clouding your mind

Time will tell if the green will become the death of society

Futuristic movies of chaos and demise will damn us all

The balance of day and night, good and evil is like a see-saw

Who will fight and accept that equality of neutral state may be achieved

Will the humbling effect become human nature or the hungry of specific beast consume us all

For people the order may be small or tall

Only time will tell the fate and the direction

Will there be a huge divide or balanced act

Talk that talk

It makes me weak in the knees

Deep moisture in the air

Slow down now

Time is on our side

Flowing and glowing with grace

Smile and be happy

It does its thing

Weight

Curves, slim, hips, asses (small, big, fake, no), boobs (small, big, fake, no) ups and downs

Unattractive, Attractive, Flawed, Beautiful

Lows, Highs, In-betweens, So-so

Harsh, Cruel, Ashamed, Delighted

Excitement, Realization, Frustration, Happiness, Sad

In-shape, Unfit, Healthy, Overweight

Stretch marks, No marks, Lines, Blemishes

Criticized, Accepted, Denial

Somewhere in the middle, in-between

Eventually Smiling

What is Love?

Love is the way my hand sweats

When I'm about to hold your hand

Love is my heart beating faster

When I'm in your arms

Love is color blind

Love is the kind words you say to me when I'm upset, nervous, scared and happy and everything in between

Love is speaking the truth even when you don't want to hear them

Love is being your biggest fan through the triumphs and failures

Love is remembering the good the bad the ugly

Love is being by your side and fighting for you

Love is respecting you as a person and accepting all of the imperfections within you and me

Love is compilation of the greatest hits the so-so and the bad songs

Love is how you feel towards the people in your life

Love is defined by so many traits

Love shouldn't pass you by if you truly understand the wonders it may bring you

Why Ask Why

Why are we failing our kids, family, etc.?

Why don't we invoke change for all people of color that includes white (if they want to change or make a difference)?

Why are we afraid of a person with brains especially a black person?

Why do some black people don't want to see other blacks succeed

Why don't we think about making black lives better?

Why can't we reach the motto of I have Dream speech?

Why we fear a strong black woman?

Why do we treat women unfairly and belittle them?

Why do a person feel vindicated when they wait till their opponent is in a lesser form?

Why do we talk to each other in a negative way?

Why is there an issue if I'm speaking the truth…is it because I'm not a yes person?

Why is there an issue to teach our children that they can do anything like got to college?

Why is there an issue if I want my child to choose a college outside of HBCU especially if I know they can compete with others outside of their race?

Why ask Why cont.

Why does a person say I'm real knowing that isn't true?

Why do some people idolize these celebrities…do you not understand that they are the popular kids in high school that have far more problems than you?

Why do black women mess with their physical appearances when they are beautiful?

Why do white women mess with their physical appearance to stay looking young?

Why can't people have a dialogue about race, sex, etc.?

Why do we let the law enforcement, judges, politicians, etc. feel they are about the law?

Why don't we look after our elderly, young, hungry, homeless, veterans, etc.?

Why do you have to play dumb to get somewhere?

Why do rich, poor, middle class people try to get on over on the system to succeed?

Why new generations of children think someone owes them something?

Why has the good music gone to the dogs?

Why can't people read between the lines, the lies and the bullshit?

Why aren't there more women CEO's but they are good enough to play house, the other woman, baby mothers, etc.

Why ask Why cont.

Why are boys and men sagging in their jeans, pants, shorts (do they think it is cute)?

Why do girls and women condone this sagging in the clothes behavior…why not enforce the change?

Why do some boys and men lie about their sexuality to girls and women and to themselves?

Why does it matter what your religion is?

Why does it matter what your sexual orientation is?

Why does it matter about your skin color?

Why can't democrats, republicans, independents or whatever get along to make policy for the people (some of them hang out together and get along when not at work)?

Why are their starving children in the United States?

Why there are no jobs for people but CEOs, companies keep getting richer?

Why are there all these one and done in college but no common or book sense to stop their accountant from cheating them out of money?

Why do we talk about the American dream but do you know what it means to you?

Why have we gotten relax on education and discipline?

Why ask Why cont.

Why do some mothers fear their children when we brought

them in this world?

Why can't some children read or write at their grade level?

Why is being ignorant the new norm?

There are a lot of why questions we should be holding not just

others but ourselves accountable. The discussions should be held and the

listening ears should be cleaned to hear and grasp. Stop being ignorant,

ask the questions and start to make a difference.

Mirror

What do you see?

Is it ugliness or prettiness?

Misshape, out of shape, perfect shape, unbelievable shape

Do you see tucks and pulls, bags, lines, spots, wrinkles

What do you see?

Is it a reflection of you?

Is there someone else you see?

Does he/she represent who you want to be or posing to be?

What do you see?

The outfit, lipstick, lashes, eye shadow

Does it look nice

Does it fit well

Is it date night, party night, work, everyday wear?

Do you present well?

 Does this reflect what you want the world to see?

WHAT DO YOU SEE??

White Girl

Because I'm not hood or ghetto

Why should that make me less black

Do you know what it means to be black

Should there be a definition

Because I diverse and like a multitude of different things

Because I'm a little refine does that make me less black

Black is Beautiful

Black is Strong

Black is Smart

Black is Colorful

Black is Mysterious

Black is Feared

Black is Envied

Black comes and goes

Black is always going to be around

Black is so many things

It is defined in everyday culture and life

So call me that white girl if it suites you but you just don't know or care to realize Black is not just hood or ghetto it is defined in multitude of ways. Maybe you need to realize or open your eyes to see what Black truly is and means.

Relaxation

Wind blowing

Cool breeze

Birds chirping

Relaxing the mind, body, soul

Inner Strength

Perseverance

Fight

Strong

Battle those demons

Stand

Head up and ^{High}

Willingness

Users

People who have their own agenda

Don't care about you

Won't to win at all cost

Everyday People

Why should they care

How many do you find?

Where in the World

Common

Understanding

Knowledge

Mind

Ignorance

Shameful

Tolerance

Complications

Sense

Neutral

Bias

Humanity

Evolution

Bliss

Eclectic

Styles

Methods

Unique

Different

Vibe

Where in the World cont.

Taste

Universal

Smooth

Mellow

Tempo

Fast

Slow

Various

Special

Bold

Entertaining

Amusing

Me, Myself, I

I stand tall

I am proud

I am beautiful

I am difficult

I am amusing

Myself is colorful

Myself is sensual

Myself is emotional

Myself is caring

Myself is educated

Me carries the weight on my shoulders

Me handles the trials and tribulations

Me deals with the bullshit

Me guides those needing guidance

Me fights the battles

Me, Myself, I work together

Me, Myself, I cry together

Me, Myself, I love together

Me, Myself, I take on the world together

Me, Myself, I

Eye of the Beholder

Visions

Color

Color Blind

Black and White

See

Blind

Half-Blind

Images

Blinking

Misses

Interpret

Channel

Bump, Bump

Pound, Pound

Thrust

Love Eternal

Bump, Pound

Pain

Slows Down

Love Everlasting

Still

Normal

Bump, Bump

Truth

Truth be told

Truth be told

Truth unveils

Truth unveils

Truth uncovers

Truth uncovers

Truth hurts

Truth hurts

Truth in knowing

Truth in knowing

Truth be told

Truth be told

Waiting

Anticipating

Relishes

Unraveling

Wrenching

Consuming

Mind-blogging

Exhausting

Treacherous

Contemplating

Denial

Gut-wrenching

Realization

Speechless

No words

No sound

Speak no evil

Eyes wide

Mouth shut

Words not forming but brewing in my head

Cannot utter or form a sentence

Calm and Relaxed

Eyebrows arched with contemplating my next move

No words

No sound

Speak no evil

Two Steps

Jealous Envy

Karma

Haters

Riddance

Dirt Dust Bruises

Shoulders Knees Face

Smile

Happiness

Fight

Angry

Forgiveness

Forgot

Two Steps cont.

Moving

Acceptance

Future Past

Smiling

Laughter

Understanding

Smiling

Enjoyment

In the End

FEAR IS PHYSICAL AND MENTALITY

FEAR IS STRONG AND VICIOUS

HOW DO YOU COMBAT THAT

WILL IT CONSUME YOU

WILL YOU LET IT DICTATE YOUR LIFE

FIGHT IT NO MATTER HOW MANY LOSES

CONFRONT IT

OVERCOME IT

DON'T LET IT WIN

FEAR ONLY SUCEEDS IF YOU LET IT WIN

TAKE A LEAP OF FAITH EVEN IF YOU DON'T BELIEVE

IN

FAITH

TRUST

FEAR WILL DISAPPEAR OVER TIME

Heed my words even though you think I'm crazy

I say some things that become truth then, now and later

Listen/see to what is in front of your face

I had to learn and still learning

Use my strengths/weakness to seek your courage

Fight your own demons and battles

I can't keep fighting or standing beside you

You need to stand on your own two feet

Seek courage and wisdom from my words and conviction

I won't keep responding or helping you out

It's your time to listen/see

Will you understand

Will you get it

When will your courage/strength shine thru

However long it takes

I will stand in the shadow

To let you grow

I will keep growing and be strong even when you're not

I will pass on the strength until I can't

Hopefully, you'll understand what I was doing

Colorful Thoughts

About the Author

She has a family and a vivid imagination. She decided to give writing a try and this is the end results. She believes everyone has colorful side and just turn it into whatever you decide.

www.ingramcontent.com/pod-product-compliance
Lightning Source LLC
Chambersburg PA
CBHW071349130626
46556CB00005B/2095